Goodbye Geese

by Nancy White Carlstrom

illustrated by Ed Young

Philomel Books   New York

Text copyright © 1991 by Nancy White Carlstrom
Illustrations copyright © 1991 by Ed Young
Philomel Books, a division of The Putnam & Grosset Book Group,
200 Madison Avenue, New York, NY 10016
Published simultaneously in Canada
Printed in Hong Kong by South China Printing Co. (1988) Ltd.
Book design by Nanette Stevenson
The text is set in Hiroshige.

Library of Congress Cataloging-in-Publication Data
Carlstrom, Nancy White.
Goodbye, geese / by Nancy White Carlstrom;
illustrated by Ed Young.   p.   cm.
Summary: A father describes the coming of winter
to his little girl.
ISBN 0-399-21832-7
[1. Winter—Fiction. 2. Fathers and daughters—Fiction.]
I. Young, Ed, ill. II. Title.
PZ7.C21684Go   1991   [E]—dc20
90-22316   CIP   AC

First Impression

Papa, is winter coming?

Yes, and when winter comes, she'll touch every living thing.

Does winter have fingers?

Yes, her frosty grip will tire the flowers.
Winter puts the whole garden to bed and covers it
with a fresh white blanket.

Does winter have hands?

Yes, but she never learned to turn the doorknob.
Winter tries to walk in through the cracks.

Does winter have feet?

Yes. Sometimes at night winter dances on top of the roof.
But she stops to watch the stars.

Does winter have eyes?

Yes, she has an icy stare that freezes the rivers and ponds.
When winter comes, she'll shade this place with darkness.

Does winter have a shape?

Yes, a great wide shape that blocks out the sun.
But she'll teach us how to sing.

Does winter have a voice?

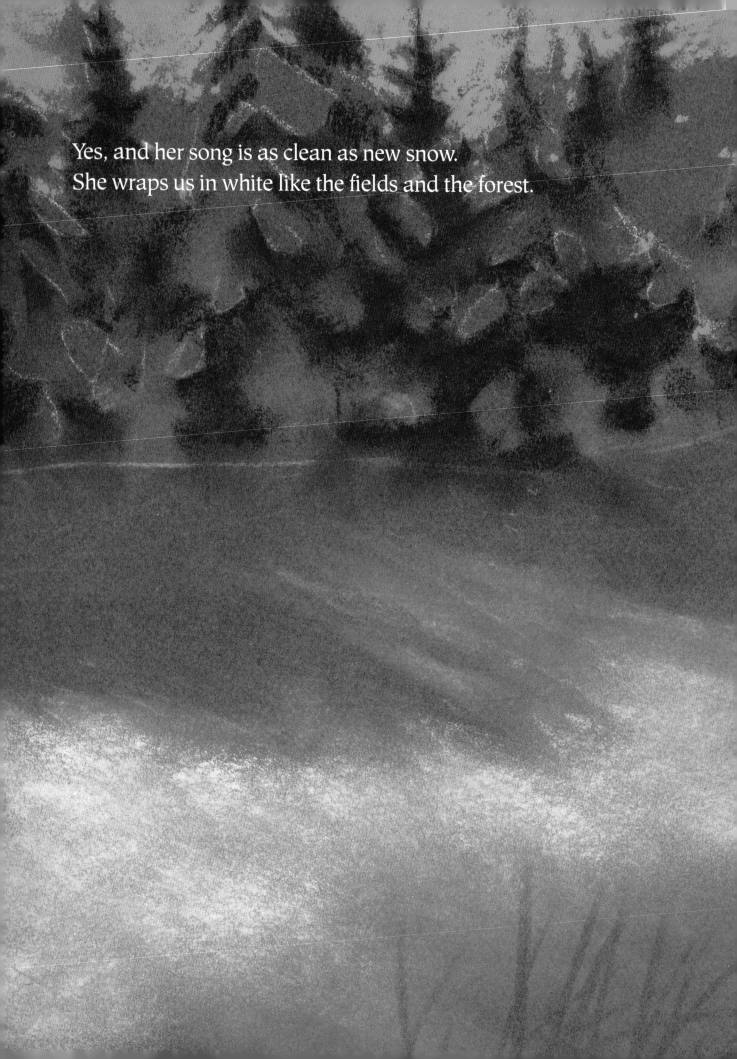

Yes, and her song is as clean as new snow.
She wraps us in white like the fields and the forest.

Does winter have arms?

Yes. Her arms are as strong as the wind's spirit,
but as quiet as the moon holding its breath.
Winter listening is everything we dream about.

Does winter have ears?

Yes, she hears even the beat of our hearts.

When geese spread their wings in the sky
and fly honking south,

winter hears
and winter comes.

Goodbye

Goodbye

Goodbye

Geese.